SADDLEBACK *Classics*

W9-BAF-451

THE
SCARLET
LETTER

NATHANIEL HAWTHORNE

ADAPTED BY

Stephen Feinstein

SADDLEBACK PUBLISHING, INC.

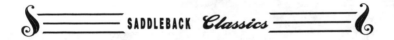

The Call of the Wild
A Christmas Carol
Frankenstein
The Adventures of Huckleberry Finn
The Red Badge of Courage
The Scarlet Letter
A Tale of Two Cities
Treasure Island

Development and Production: Laurel Associates, Inc.
Cover and Interior Art: Black Eagle Productions

SADDLEBACK PUBLISHING, INC.
3505 Cadillac Ave., Building F-9
Costa Mesa, CA 92626-1443

ISBN 1-56254-274-5

Printed in the United States of America
05 04 03 02 01 00 M 99   9 8 7 6 5 4 3 2 1

CONTENTS

1 On the Scaffold

It was a summer morning in the year 1642. In the small town of Boston, an angry crowd was gathering in front of a wooden building. Its oak door was studded with iron spikes. The building was a prison.

The people in the crowd were Puritans, people who followed a strict religious code. The men had beards and wore dark clothes and tall gray hats. The women wore white caps or cloaks with hoods. Everyone's eyes were glued to the door. They were waiting to see the prisoner, Hester Prynne.

One woman in the crowd said, "The Reverend Dimmesdale is very upset that such a scandal has come upon his church."

"The judges have shown too much mercy," said another woman. "We women would not have been so easy. At the very least, they should have put the brand of a hot iron on her forehead. As it is, she can easily cover up the mark. And then she can walk the streets as brave as ever."

Yet another woman added in an angry voice, "Why do we talk of marks and brands? This woman has brought shame upon us all. Surely she ought to die!"

"Mercy on us!" said a man in the crowd. "Those are the hardest words yet. Hush now! The lock is turning in the prison door. Here comes Mistress Prynne herself."

Stepping out into the bright morning sunshine was an official of the court. He was leading a tall young woman. As she came through the door, Hester Prynne shook free of his hand. Walking proudly, she carried a three-month-old baby in her arms. She looked around at the faces in the crowd. When she saw her neighbors, she smiled and blushed. On the front of Hester Prynne's gown, in fine red cloth, was the letter A. It was surrounded by fancy designs in gold thread. Hester was skilled at needlework. She had done the embroidery on the gown herself.

Those who knew Hester were amazed at how her beauty shone out. It was not what they had expected at a time like this. They thought she would have looked sad, as if under a dark cloud. Instead, her dark hair, deep black eyes, and beautiful features seemed to express a wild and free spirit. But the sight that drew all eyes was that scarlet letter. It had the effect of setting Hester aside from all other people.

"The hussy!" said a woman. "She uses her skill with the needle to laugh in our faces. Why, she's figured out a way to take pride in what was meant to be punishment."

"We should strip her gown from her shoulders," cried another woman.

"I'll give a piece of my old red flannel to make a more fitting letter," said a third, sour-faced woman.

The grim court official was trying to lead Hester toward the marketplace. He made a motion with his staff. "Make way, good people! Make way, in the King's name!" he cried. "Open a passage! I promise you that every man, woman, and child will get a good look at Mistress Prynne's mark of sin."

A lane was opened through the crowd. "Come along with me, Mistress Hester. Show your scarlet letter in the marketplace!" said the court official. Following behind him, Hester set forth toward the place set for her punishment.

The distance from the prison door to the marketplace was not very great. But for Hester the walk seemed to take a very long time. Schoolboys ran in front, staring up into her face. People on both sides of her shouted words such as, "Shameless woman!" Every step of the way was torture for Hester. Yet she passed through this part of her punishment with outward calm. Finally she reached the marketplace.

A scaffold had been set up at the western end of the marketplace. It stood beneath the eaves of Boston's oldest church. Hester approached the scaffold and climbed a flight of wooden steps. There she stood for everyone to see. For a moment Hester felt like crying out and throwing herself from the scaffold. Yet in the next moment the crowd of people before her seemed to disappear. Instead, she saw the people and places she had known in her childhood.

In her mind Hester saw again the village in Old England where she was born. She saw her home—the small, poor house of gray stone, now falling apart. She saw her father's face with the white beard that flowed over his collar. Her mother's face wore her typical look of love and concern.

And she saw her own face, glowing with girlish beauty, in the mirror in which she had so often looked.

There was another face in her memory— thin, pale, and intelligent. This was the face of an older man whose left shoulder was higher than his right. The man's eyes were dim from studying so many books by lamplight. Hester remembered that a new life, in connection with this strange man, had seemed to await her.

Then these shifting scenes faded. Once again Hester gazed at the marketplace. As she stood there, she wondered if all of this could really be happening to her. She held the child so tightly that it cried out in pain. She looked down at the scarlet letter and touched it. Yes! The baby and the shame were real. All else had disappeared.

2 A Familiar Face

As Hester stood holding her child on the scaffold, she wished that she could be somewhere else. To keep her mind off her suffering, she looked out over the crowd. On its outer edge, two men caught her eye—an Indian and the white man standing beside him. The white man was dressed in a strange combination of English and Indian clothes.

Hester stared at the strange white man's face. He had an intelligent expression, as though he had spent many years studying books. Then Hester noticed that one of his shoulders rose higher than the other. Suddenly she realized that she knew this man. Her eyes met his across the crowd. But as soon as the man saw that Hester recognized him, he put his finger to his lips.

Then the man touched the shoulder of a

townsman standing next to him. "Sir, who is that woman?" he asked. "Why is she set up to public shame?"

The townsman said, "Friend, you must be a stranger in this region. Or else you would have heard of Mistress Hester Prynne and her evil ways. She has raised a great scandal in Master Dimmesdale's church."

"I am indeed a stranger in these parts. I have met with misfortune on sea and on land," said the stranger. "For a long time I was held captive by the Indians south of here. This Indian with me brought me here to arrange for my ransom. Will you tell me of Hester Prynne's—am I saying her name correctly?—of this woman's crimes, what has brought her to this scaffold?"

"Truly, I will tell you, friend," said the townsman. "How glad your heart must be to find yourself here in Boston—where sin is punished. This woman was the wife of an English gentleman. He had decided to come over and join us in Massachusetts. He sent his wife here before him, staying behind to look after some business. But sir, would you believe it . . . In the two years she has been here, no word has come of her husband! And the young wife, being left all alone. . . "

"Aha! I see," said the stranger with a bitter smile. "A wise husband might have known what would happen. So who is the baby's father?"

"In truth, friend, that remains a mystery," answered the townsman. "Mistress Prynne refuses to name him."

"The husband should come himself to look into this mystery," said the stranger with a smile.

"He should, indeed—if he is still alive," said the townsman. "Most likely, he is at the bottom of the sea. That is why our good judges have not sentenced her to death. They have ordered that she stand on the scaffold for three hours. Also, she must wear the scarlet letter for the rest of her life."

"A wise sentence," said the stranger, bowing his head. "Something bothers me, however. Surely her partner in sin should, at least, stand on the scaffold by her side. Surely he will be known!—he will be known!—he will be known!"

The stranger bowed politely to the townsman. Then he and the Indian made their way through the crowd. All this time, Hester had not taken her eyes off the stranger. Now she was almost glad that she was standing on the scaffold in front of a large crowd. It would have been worse, much worse, to have had to greet the man, face to face, the two of them alone.

"Hester Prynne!" said a stern voice. Hester was so lost in thought that at first she didn't hear her name. "Listen, Hester Prynne!" the voice said, loudly.

Hester looked up. It was John Wilson, the oldest minister in Boston. He was standing on a balcony, directly above the scaffold. Some of Boston's most important citizens, including Governor Bellingham, were with him. Wilson put his hand on the shoulder of a pale young man beside him. "I've asked my young friend Mr. Dimmesdale to talk to you before all of the people here. As your pastor, perhaps he can get you to tell us who led you into this sin. He didn't want to, but now I'm asking him once again. Brother Dimmesdale, will it be you or I that shall deal with this poor sinner's soul?"

Then the Governor said, "Good Master Dimmesdale, you must somehow persuade this woman to repent and confess. You are responsible now for this woman's soul." This direct appeal drew the eyes of the whole crowd to the Reverend Arthur Dimmesdale. The young clergyman had come from one of England's greatest universities. He had already become known for his skill as a speaker and for his strong religious feelings. Now he stepped forward. His face had gone white and his lips shook. He seemed very nervous and frightened.

"Hester Prynne," he said, "if you feel it will bring peace to your soul, I ask you to speak the name of your fellow sinner and fellow sufferer. Do not be silent from any mistaken pity for him. Believe me, Hester, it would be good if he were to step down from a high place to stand beside you. That would be better than to hide a guilty heart for the rest of his life."

The young pastor's voice was sweet, rich, deep, and heartfelt. People seemed to be moved more by the sound of his voice than by his words. Dimmesdale's voice brought out feelings of sympathy in the hearts of all who listened. Even Hester's poor baby felt the influence of that fine voice. Holding up its little arms, the baby looked toward Dimmesdale. The people in the crowd now felt that Hester would surely speak the sinner's name.

But Hester shook her head.

"Woman!" Reverend Wilson cried in a harsh voice. "Speak out the name! Just tell us the name and repent—and you will be allowed to remove the scarlet letter."

"Never!" said Hester. As she said this, she looked not at Wilson but into the eyes of the young minister.

"*Speak*, woman!" cried out another voice from the crowd about the scaffold. "Speak, and give your child a father!"

"I will not speak!" answered Hester. Having recognized this stern voice, she had turned pale as death. "My child must seek a heavenly Father. She shall never know an earthly one."

"She will not speak," Dimmesdale said softly. He had been leaning over the balcony, with his hand upon his heart. Like everyone else, he had been waiting for Hester's answer. Now he stood up and said to himself, "What a wonderful woman. She is so strong and has such a generous heart. She will not speak!"

So Hester Prynne remained on the scaffold. Reverend Wilson began a long sermon, warning about the evils of sin. He kept coming back to the scarlet letter. Hester's baby began to cry, but Hester wasn't able to quiet her. Finally, with her secret still her own, Hester was led down from the scaffold and returned to prison.

3 The Interview

After being led back to prison, Hester Prynne's nerves were on edge. She began to act in strange ways. Her baby cried much of the time. Master Brackett, the jailer, was afraid that Hester might harm herself or the baby. He brought in a doctor, whom he introduced as Dr. Roger Chillingworth.

Hester became as still as death, although the baby continued to moan. Chillingworth was the same man Hester had recognized in the crowd by the scaffold.

"Leave me alone with my patient," the doctor said to the jailer. "Trust me—it shall soon be peaceful in your prison."

Chillingworth examined the baby carefully. Then he took some medicine out of a leather case. He mixed the medicine with water in a cup. "I've learned a lot about medicine from my studies and my stay with the Indians. Here, woman. This child is yours, not mine. Give the baby this medicine with your own hand."

Hester looked into the doctor's face with questioning eyes. She did not trust Chillingworth. "Would you take revenge on an innocent baby?" she whispered.

"Foolish woman!" said the doctor. "Why would I want to harm your baby? I would give this medicine even if it were my own child." Chillingworth took the baby in his arms and gave it the medicine. Soon his little patient stopped moaning and fell into a deep sleep.

Next, the doctor examined Hester. He felt her pulse and looked into her eyes. His gaze made her heart shrink and shudder. It was very familiar, yet so strange and cold. Now Chillingworth prepared some medicine for Hester. "Drink this; it will calm you. It is from a recipe taught to me by an Indian."

"I have thought about death, even wished for it," said Hester. "Yet if death is in this cup, I ask you to think again before I drink it." Hester studied his eyes.

"Drink, then," the doctor said. "Do you know me so little? Even if I wanted revenge, what could be better than to let you live?"

Hester drank the medicine in the cup. "Hester," the doctor went on, "it was my own foolishness that led to your troubles. What had I—an old man interested only in books and ideas—to do with youth and beauty like your own? Had I really been wise, I might have foreseen all of this."

"You know I was honest with you," said Hester. "I never pretended to love you."

"True. It was my fault, as I've said. But I was lonely. It didn't seem so wild a dream at the time. As old as I was, I still believed I could find happiness. I wanted to get married and have a family."

"I fear I have greatly wronged you," said Hester.

"We have wronged each other," said the doctor. "And now we are even. I seek no revenge against you. But the man lives who has wronged us both. You must tell me his name, Hester. Who is he?"

"Do not ask me this," answered Hester, looking firmly into Chillingworth's face. "You shall never know!"

"You will not reveal his name? I will find him anyway. Let him live! Let him hide himself, if he may! But one day he shall be mine!" the doctor cried. "Now there is one thing I must ask of you," he went on. "As you have kept his secret, now keep mine. Tell no one I am your husband!"

"But why do you ask this?" said Hester. "Why not announce it yourself, and get rid of me at once?"

"It may be that I do not want to be known as a husband who has been betrayed by his wife," Chillingworth said. "It may be for other reasons. But that is my business. Therefore, let the world believe that your husband is already dead. Above all, tell not a word of our secret to the man you are protecting. If you should fail me in this, beware! His life will be in my hands."

"Very well then. I will keep your secret, as I have his," said Hester.

"Swear it!" the doctor demanded.

Hester did so. Then the doctor gathered his things and got ready to leave. He said, "And now, Mistress Prynne, I leave you alone with your baby and the scarlet letter. And perhaps your bad dreams." He had a strange, unpleasant smile on his face.

Hester didn't like the look of that smile. "Why are you smiling like this?" she said. "Have you made me promise something that will ruin my soul?"

"Not *your* soul, Hester. No, not yours!" And with those words, Chillingworth left the room.

§ 4 Pearl

The day finally came when Hester's prison term ended. The prison door was thrown open. Hester, carrying her little child, stepped out into the bright sunshine. It was a beautiful day, the sort of day that makes people feel happy to be alive. Although Hester was indeed glad to be free of prison, she was not free from the sickness in her heart. To her, it seemed as if the sun's only purpose was to shine on the scarlet letter on her dress.

Now that she had served her time in prison, Hester was free to go where she pleased. She could have gone back to England, or anywhere else. But in her heart she did not feel free. She felt that she must remain in Boston and continue to wear the scarlet letter. She believed that she had not

yet finished paying for her sin.

Hester got permission from the judges to move into a little cottage on the edge of town. The house sat on a lonely bluff overlooking the sea. Here she lived with her child, little Pearl. To earn a living, Hester did needlework for the women in town. Before long, word of her skill spread and her work was in demand. People paid her to sew decorations on their scarves, caps, and gloves. But no one ever asked her to work on a white bridal veil.

Hester had no friends. Although she was kind to others, people were often cruel to her. People would point to her in the street. Children would call her names and run after her. When she went to church, the pastor would make her the topic of the sermon. Because she had nobody to help take care of little Pearl, Hester and her child were never apart.

Hester had named the child "Pearl," as a jewel of great price. Pearl had cost Hester a great deal indeed. Still, the baby was her only treasure.

One day Hester was bending over Pearl's cradle. The baby looked up and noticed the gold on the letter A. She put up her little hand and grabbed the letter, laughing. The scarlet letter thus became the first object that Pearl had ever noticed.

As Pearl grew, she never made friends among the other children. She was just as much an outcast among the Puritans as was her mother. Pearl seemed to sense that the adults did not want her to play with their children. So she saw them as enemies. She never tried to speak to the other children. If they ever gathered around her, she would chase them and throw stones at them.

Pearl enjoyed playing among the pine trees at home. She imagined the trees were Puritans, and she laughed at them. The ugly weeds in the garden became Puritan children, whom she struck down.

Pearl was growing into a beautiful and intelligent little girl. She had a wild spirit and a love of mischief, and Hester could not control her. One day Pearl invented a new game. She gathered up a bunch of wild flowers. Then she began throwing flowers at the scarlet letter on her mother's dress. Laughing, Pearl danced up and down like a little devil. She had a strange look in her eyes that frightened Hester.

"Child, what are you?" cried the mother.

"Oh, I am your little Pearl!" answered the child, laughing.

"You are not my child! You are no Pearl of mine," said Hester, half playfully, half sadly. "Tell me, then, what are you and who sent you here?"

"You tell *me*, mother," said the child, seriously. She came up to Hester and pressed herself close to her knees. "Do tell me!"

"Why, the Heavenly Father sent you!" answered Hester.

Pearl reached up and touched the scarlet letter with a small fingertip. "No, he did not send me," the little girl cried. "I have no Heavenly Father!"

"Hush, Pearl! You must not talk like this!" said the mother. "He sent us all into this world, even me, your mother. If he did not send you, then from where did you come?"

"Tell me! Tell me!" repeated Pearl, no longer serious. She was laughing and rolling on the floor. "It is you who must tell me!"

Hester thought for a long time, but could not give her daughter an answer. She did not know the answer to that question.

5 At the Governor's House

One day Hester Prynne went to the house of Governor Bellingham. She was bringing him a pair of fine gloves that she had embroidered. These elegant gloves were to be worn for special occasions.

There was another and more important reason for Hester's visit, however. Hester had heard that the Governor and others thought that her child should be taken from her. They thought that she was not a good mother for Pearl. The little girl, who was already three years old, would be better off being raised by other people.

On this day, Hester had dressed Pearl in a red velvet dress decorated with gold thread. Pearl's dress looked a lot like the scarlet letter on Hester's dress. As Hester and Pearl made their way down the street toward the Governor's house, they passed a group of children.

"Look!" cried a boy. "There is the woman of the scarlet letter. And there is the likeness of the scarlet letter running by her side. Let's throw mud at them."

When Pearl heard this, she screamed and shouted at the children. She stamped her foot and shook her fist. Frightened by the little girl rushing at them, the Puritan children ran away. At that, Pearl smiled sweetly at her mother. The two reached the Governor's house without further adventure.

One of the Governor's servants met them at the front door. "Good day. Is the Governor home?" asked Hester.

"He is, but he has visitors—some ministers and a doctor. You may not see him now," said the servant.

"Nevertheless, I will enter," said Hester. She stepped inside, Pearl following right behind her. Because of Hester's proud manner, the servant thought she must be a person of some importance. So he didn't try to stop her.

Inside the hall, they came across the Governor's suit of armor. The polished steel shone like a mirror. Pearl was pleased with the armor. She spent some time looking at it.

"Mother," Pearl cried, "I see you here. Look! Look!"

Hester looked. She saw that, because the reflection was curved, the scarlet letter looked huge. In fact Hester appeared to be hidden behind it. "Come along, Pearl!" she said, drawing her away. "Come and look at this garden outside the window."

Pearl, seeing rosebushes, began to beg for a red rose.

"Hush, child, hush!" said her mother. "Do not cry, dear little Pearl! I hear voices in the garden. The Governor is coming, and some gentlemen along with him."

Turning to look, Pearl saw some men approaching, and became silent. The Governor was walking with Reverend Wilson. Behind them came Reverend Dimmesdale and Doctor Chillingworth.

"Well, well, what have we here?" said the Governor when he saw Pearl.

"Indeed," said Reverend Wilson, "what little bird of scarlet may this be? Are you a Christian child?"

"I am my mother's child," answered the little girl in red, "and my name is Pearl."

"But where is your mother?" asked the old minister. "Ah! I see," he added. Turning to the Governor, he whispered, "This is the child about whom we were just speaking . . . and her unhappy mother, Hester Prynne."

"We might have guessed that her mother must be the scarlet woman!" said the Governor. "Let us look into this matter."

Governor Bellingham stepped into the hall, followed by his three guests. "Hester Prynne," said the Governor, "there has been much talk about the child. Wouldn't it be better for her if she were taken from you? She should be dressed properly. And she needs to be taught manners and the truths of heaven and earth. What can a poor woman like you do for the child?"

"I can teach my little Pearl what I have learned from this," said Hester, pointing to the scarlet letter.

"Woman, it is your badge of shame! It is because of that letter that we would put the child into other hands!" said the Governor.

"But the letter teaches me lessons each day," Hester added. "From these lessons my child may become wiser and better."

"We shall see," said the Governor. "Good Master Wilson, please see if this child has learned what a good Christian of her age should know."

Mr. Wilson sat down in a chair next to the little girl. "Pearl," he said, "can you tell me, my child, who made you?"

Pearl knew who had made her. Her mother had taught her all about the Father in heaven. But this is not what she told Mr. Wilson. Instead, the little girl said that she had been picked by her mother from a bush of wild roses.

Old Roger Chillingworth smiled and turned to whisper something in Reverend Dimmesdale's ear. Hester looked at the doctor. He looked even more ugly than she remembered him to be.

"This is awful!" cried the Governor in

shock. "Here is a three-year-old child, and she cannot tell who made her! Gentlemen, we need ask no more questions."

Hester grabbed Pearl and drew her into her arms. "God gave me this child," she cried. "She is my happiness—and she is my torture! Pearl keeps me here in life! Pearl punishes me, too! You shall not take her! I will die first!"

"My poor woman," said Mr. Wilson, "the child shall be well cared for! Far better than you can do!"

"It was God who gave the child into my keeping," repeated Hester. Her voice had risen almost to a scream. "I will not give her up." Then she turned to Mr. Dimmesdale for the first time. "Speak for me," she cried. "You were my pastor. You know me better than these men can. You know what is in my heart. I will not lose the child. *Help* me!"

Dimmesdale stepped forward. The pale young man held his hand over his heart. Hester noticed that he always did this when he was nervous. And Dimmesdale looked as though his health was failing. He had lost weight. She saw a look of pain and sadness in his large dark eyes.

"There is truth in what she says," began the minister. His sweet yet powerful voice shook as he spoke. "God gave Hester the child as a blessing—the one blessing in her life! Also, as she has told us, God has meant to punish her. She has shown this in the dress of the poor child. It is to remind us of what the red letter stands for."

"Well said!" cried Mr. Wilson. "I was afraid the woman had no better thought than to make a clown of the child."

"Oh, not so!" cried Dimmesdale. "Hester knows what the child was meant by God to do. It is to keep her from falling into sin again. For her sake—no less than for the child's—let us leave them as God has placed them."

"Ah, you speak with strong feeling, my friend," said the old doctor, smiling at Dimmesdale.

"And there is much truth in what he says," added Mr. Wilson. "What do *you* say, Master Bellingham? Has he not pleaded well for the poor woman?"

"Indeed he has," said the Governor. "We will leave the matter as it stands—so long as there is no further scandal."

Pearl ran up to Reverend Dimmesdale. She took his hand in both of hers, and put her cheek against it. Dimmesdale put his hand on the girl's head and kissed her brow. Then Pearl ran laughing and dancing down the long hall.

"A strange child," said the old doctor. "It is easy to see her mother in her. Suppose we were to watch her closely. Do you think it might then be possible to guess who the father is?"

"No, it would be sinful," said Mr. Wilson. "Surely it is better to pray on it and leave the mystery as we find it. Let every good Christian man show a father's kindness toward the poor child."

Hester and Pearl then left the house. As they were going down the stairs, a voice above them said, "Hist! Hist! Hssst!"

They looked up. In an open window was the face of Mistress Hibbins, the Governor's sister. She was known as a mean old woman.

Several years later, Mistress Hibbins would be put to death as a witch. In those days, of course, people believed in witches.

Mistress Hibbins said, "Will you go with us tonight? There will be a merry company in the forest. I promised the Devil that Hester Prynne would be there!"

"Please make my excuse to him," Hester answered with a smile. "I must stay home and care for my little Pearl. Had they taken her from me, I would have gladly gone with you. And I would have signed my name in the Devil's book—with my own blood!"

"We shall have you there soon," said the witch-lady, as she drew back her head.

§6 The Doctor and His Patient

Reverend Arthur Dimmesdale was loved and much admired by the members of his church. They had noticed that the young pastor's health had begun to fail. Therefore, they were very happy that Dr. Roger Chillingworth had dropped into their lives. Some even felt this to be an act of God. Yet each Sunday, Reverend Dimmesdale seemed to be paler and thinner, and his voice grew weaker.

The people believed that Chillingworth, with his great knowledge of medicine, would be able to save their beloved pastor. Nobody knew why Chillingworth had shown up in Boston at this time. After all, why would a great doctor from a German university choose to settle in Boston? The only explanation for this miracle must be that he had been sent to care for Reverend Dimmesdale.

The elders of the church arranged for Chillingworth to care for Dimmesdale. "His health is getting worse," they said to the old doctor. "But with your fine care he is sure to be healed. No doubt it is God's will that you should care for him."

Then the elders went to speak to Dimmesdale about his health. They urged him to accept Chillingworth's help.

"I need no medicine," said Dimmesdale.

"Do you wish to die? Don't you know it would be a sin to refuse the help that God has offered? It is your duty to get well. Your people need you," said the church elders.

Dimmesdale listened in silence. Then he said, "Were it God's will that my life end today, I would be content."

Chillingworth then spoke out. "Young clergymen often seem too willing to give up their hold of life. It is as if they would rather walk with God in heaven."

"No," said Dimmesdale, putting his hand to his heart. He looked as if he were in pain.

"Were I more worthy to walk *there*, I could be happier to work *here*."

"Good men always judge themselves too harshly," said Chillingworth.

In this manner, Chillingworth became Dimmesdale's doctor. The old doctor was not only interested in the young pastor's medical problems. He wanted to learn as much as he could about Dimmesdale as a person. As time went on, the two men became friends. They spent more and more time together. People saw them taking long walks on the seashore and in the forest. They had long talks about everything—great ideas, nature, history.

Finally, at Chillingworth's suggestion, the two agreed to share the same house. In this way the doctor could keep a constant watch over his patient. Dimmesdale had an apartment in front. On the other side of the house, Chillingworth set up his laboratory.

As the years went by, people began to see a change in Dr. Chillingworth. When they looked at his face, they could see something evil and ugly they had not noticed before.

At the same time, Dimmesdale had not gotten well. If anything, he had become more troubled. He often had nightmares— sometimes he saw devils, sometimes angels. And there was often a look of terror and gloom in his eyes.

Some people began to suspect that Chillingworth was either an agent of the Devil or the Devil himself. They wondered if their young pastor was being tested in some way by God. And they prayed that he would some day win out in this terrible battle for his soul.

Dimmesdale still did not know that Dr. Chillingworth was his enemy. He was not aware that Chillingworth was trying to pry loose his secret. Although he did not entirely trust the old doctor, he did not completely trust *any* man. So he continued to treat Chillingworth in a friendly manner.

Then one day Dimmesdale was watching the doctor at work in his laboratory. Chillingworth was looking at some odd-looking leaves. He was studying them to see if they could be used as a medicine.

Dimmesdale asked where he had gotten the leaves. The doctor said he had found them in the graveyard. They were growing from a dead man's heart.

"These leaves may represent some awful secret that was buried with him," said Chillingworth. "Perhaps the poor man would have been better off confessing during his lifetime."

"It may be that he *wished* to but could not," said the pastor. "Anyway, on judgment day all secrets will be told. Those who tell the truth will be free at last and filled with joy."

"Then why should the guilty not tell their secrets here and now?" asked the doctor.

"Some men could no longer do God's work on earth if others knew their secrets," said Dimmesdale. Saying this, he put his hand on his chest, as if to stop a sudden pain.

"Ah, but such men lie to themselves," said Chillingworth. "Would you have me believe that living a lie can be better than God's own truth? Trust me, dear sir, such men lie to themselves."

"It may be so," said the young clergyman.

His tone of voice showed that he was no longer interested in the topic.

Several days later, Chillingworth found Dimmesdale sitting in his chair. Having been reading, the pastor had fallen into a deep sleep. Chillingworth quietly went up to him and pulled open his shirt. The old doctor stared in wonder at the young man's chest. When he turned away, a wild look of joy and horror was on his face. Anyone seeing Chillingworth's face at this moment would have seen a face like the Devil's.

From that day on, Chillingworth was driven by the desire for revenge. Without knowing why, Dimmesdale came to hate and fear the old man. After all, the doctor always spoke to him with kindness. He seemed to care about his health. But Chillingworth had started to deliberately say things to remind Dimmesdale of his sin.

The more the church members noticed how much Dimmesdale suffered, the more they loved him. When he said that he was a sinner, people called him a saint. But Dimmesdale knew that he was living a lie.

He hated himself for deceiving them. Yet he could not bring himself to do the one thing that would free him—confess his sin. So he continued to suffer, tortured by his own thoughts. And he was beginning to have trouble sleeping at night.

7 A Sign in the Night Sky

It was a dark and cloudy night in early May. Reverend Dimmesdale was tossing and turning in his bed. While his usual unhappy thoughts were going through his mind, a new idea came to him. Maybe it would help bring him some peace of mind. Dimmesdale got dressed and quietly left the house. He walked as if in the shadow of a dream. Soon he reached the scaffold where Hester Prynne had stood seven years ago.

Now Dimmesdale stood on the scaffold. He said to himself, "The town is asleep. No one can see me—it means nothing." Suddenly he shouted out in agony. His cry went ringing through the night. Afraid that the whole town would rush out and find him there, Dimmesdale covered his face and waited for people to come running.

But no one came. The townspeople did not awake. Then a light came on in the windows of Governor Bellingham's house. The Governor looked out the window. Mistress Hibbins stuck her head out of another window. But they couldn't see anyone in the darkness. So they put out their lights and went back to bed.

A short while later, Dimmesdale saw someone coming up the street carrying a lantern. It was the Reverend Wilson. He had just left the deathbed of old Governor Winthrop. Dimmesdale could not stop himself from calling out a greeting. But the Reverend didn't hear him. He passed by and kept going up the street.

Dimmesdale laughed in relief. And a child's laugh answered him! It sounded like little Pearl's voice.

"Pearl! Little Pearl!" he cried. "Hester! Hester Prynne! Are you there?"

"Yes, it is Hester Prynne!" the woman replied in a tone of surprise. "It is I, and my little Pearl."

"What are you doing here at this late

hour?" said Reverend Dimmesdale.

"I have been watching at Governor Winthrop's deathbed. They called me to take his measure for a burial robe. Now we are on our way home," said Hester.

"Come up here, Hester and Pearl," said Dimmesdale. "You have both been on the scaffold before, but I was not with you. Come up here once again, and we will stand all three together!"

Hester silently climbed the steps. She stood on the scaffold, holding little Pearl by the hand. The minister took the child's other hand. A rush of new life seemed to pour into his heart and veins. It was as if the three of them formed an electric chain.

"Minister, will you stand here with mother and me, tomorrow at noon?" asked Pearl.

"No, my little Pearl," answered the minister. "Another time, but not tomorrow."

Pearl laughed and tried to pull away her hand. But the minister held it tight. "A moment longer, my child!" he said.

"But will you promise," asked Pearl,

"to take hold of my hand, and my mother's hand, tomorrow at noon?"

"Not then, Pearl," said the minister, "but another time!"

"And what other time?" Pearl asked.

"At the great judgment day!" whispered the minister. "Then and there, before God, your good mother and you and I must stand together! But the daylight of this world shall not see our meeting!"

But before Dimmesdale had finished speaking, a light filled the sky. No doubt it was caused by a meteor. The strange light made the street as bright as day. As the meteor's light burned through the clouds, Dimmesdale looked up. At that moment he thought he saw a giant letter A in the sky. It seemed to be marked in lines of dull red light. Of course, the young minister was the only one to see such a sight.

Just then, Dimmesdale noticed that Pearl was pointing her finger at someone coming toward them. It was old Roger Chillingworth! "Who is that man, Hester?" he gasped. "There is something terribly evil about him. Do you know that man? I *hate* him, Hester!"

Hester was silent. She remembered her promise to Chillingworth not to reveal that she knew him.

"Minister," said Pearl. "I can tell you who he is!" She whispered something in Dimmesdale's ear. But she was only making childish sounds that did not mean anything.

"What, child? Are you making fun of me?" said Dimmesdale.

"You were not honest," answered the child. "You would not promise to take my hand and my mother's hand at noon tomorrow."

"Master Dimmesdale!" called out the old doctor. "Can that be you? Men like us, whose heads are in our books, need to be looked after. We dream while awake, and walk in our sleep! Come, my dear friend, let me take you home."

"How did you know I was here?" asked Dimmesdale in a frightened, haunted voice.

"I didn't," said Chillingworth. "I was at the deathbed of Governor Winthrop. After he died, I was on my way home. Now come with me, or you will hardly be able to speak in church tomorrow. These books! These books! How they trouble the brain. You study too much. Come with me now."

Dimmesdale nodded sadly. "I will go home with you." Giving in to the doctor, he allowed himself to be led away.

8   Hester and the Doctor

Over the course of seven years, the people of Boston had changed their minds about Hester. She had earned the respect of the community. By doing her work well, she earned a living for herself and Pearl. She never complained when treated badly. Nobody was more willing to give to the poor. And when there was illness or trouble, she always brought help and comfort.

On the night of their strange meeting on the scaffold, Hester had been shocked at Dimmesdale's condition. She was afraid of what the old doctor might do to him. Now she was better able to deal with Chillingworth than she was seven years ago. By facing up to her problems, she had grown strong over the years. At last she decided the time had come to talk to her former husband. She would do all in her power to rescue Dimmesdale from the evil grip of the old doctor.

One afternoon Hester came upon Chillingworth when she was walking with Pearl by the seashore. The old doctor had a basket in one arm and a staff in the other. He was bent over the ground, looking for roots and herbs with which to make medicines. Hester told her daughter to go play by the water's edge.

"I would speak a word with you," Hester said to the doctor.

"Ah! And is it Mistress Hester that has a word for old Roger Chillingworth?" he answered. Standing up straight, he said, "Why, I hear such good things about you. In fact, I asked the judges if they might allow you to stop wearing the scarlet letter."

"It's not up to them to take off this letter," replied Hester. "If I deserved to be rid of it, it would fall away by itself."

"Well then, wear it—if it suits you better," said Chillingworth coldly. "A woman needs to dress as she pleases."

As they spoke, Hester looked carefully at the old doctor. She was shocked at the change that had come over him in the past seven years. It was not so much that he had grown older. But his thirst for revenge seemed to have turned him into a devil. His eyes seemed to glow with an evil red light—as if his soul were on fire! After all, this unhappy person had taken pleasure in watching another man suffer.

"What do you see in my face that makes you stare so?" asked Chillingworth.

"Something that would make me weep, if there were any tears bitter enough for it," she answered. "But let it pass. It is of the minister that I would speak."

"What of him?" said the doctor. "It is true that he is always in my thoughts. So speak freely and I will answer you."

"Sir, when you and I spoke together in prison seven years ago," said Hester, "you made me swear to keep secret that you had been my husband."

"What choice did you have?" asked Chillingworth. "My finger pointed at this man would have gotten him thrown into prison. Perhaps even hanged!"

"For Dimmesdale that might have been better!" cried Hester.

"What evil have I done the man?" asked the doctor. "I tell you, Hester, the richest king could not afford the care I have wasted on this miserable priest! It is thanks to me alone that he still walks upon this earth."

"Better had he died at once!" cried Hester. "Each day you make him die a living death. You look into his mind! You dig into his heart! You walk behind every step he takes!"

"Ah, yes, you are so right!" laughed Chillingworth. "Never has a man suffered more than he! And all in the sight of his worst enemy! He believes it is the Devil who tortures him. He never suspects that it is his own doctor!"

"Have you not tortured him enough?" asked Hester.

"No, not *nearly* enough!" cried the old doctor. "Do you remember what I used to be like? Was I not a kind and good person? Now look at me. I have become evil. And all because of the wrong that was done me."

"Now I must reveal the secret," said Hester. "It is time he knew who you are. Time that he knew the man always at his side is his enemy. I must tell him—no matter *what* you do! This way is no good for him, no good for me, no good for you! And it is no good for little Pearl!"

The old man looked at Hester. "If only you had found a better love than mine," he said sadly, "this evil would not have happened! Hester, I pity you for the good that has been wasted in you!"

"And I pity *you* for the hatred that has turned a wise and good man into an evil man," said Hester.

"You are not sinful, Hester—and I am not evil," said Chillingworth. "It is our fate. You may go and say whatever you wish to the minister." Then the old doctor went on his way, bending down here and there to pick up an herb or root.

As she watched him go, Hester said to herself, "I hate the man!" She knew it was wrong to hate. But she could not stop herself from feeling this way. Once he was gone, she called out to her child. "Pearl! Little Pearl! Where are you?"

Pearl came dancing and laughing up from the beach. She was wearing an ornament she had made out of seaweed. It was in the shape of a letter A—a green letter A. "Pearl, your green letter has no purpose. But do you know why your mother wears this letter?"

"Truly I do," answered Pearl, looking into her mother's face. "It is for the same reason that the minister keeps his hand over his heart!"

"And what reason is that?" asked Hester. "What has the letter to do with any heart except mine?"

"I have told you all I know," said Pearl. "Ask that old man who was here with you. Maybe he can tell. But really, Mother, what does this scarlet letter mean? And why does the minister keep his hand over his heart?" She took her mother's hand in both of her own. Then she gazed with a serious look into her mother's eyes.

Pearl repeated her questions. Hester

remained silent, not sure how to respond. Finally she said, "Silly Pearl, what questions are these? There are many things in this world that a child must not ask about. What do I know about the minister's heart? And as for the scarlet letter, I wear it because of its gold thread."

Several more times that day, Pearl asked Hester the same questions. Then she asked again just before going to sleep. And she asked again as soon as she woke up the next morning. Finally Hester said, "Be quiet, child! Do not bother me or I will shut you into a dark closet!"

9   A Meeting in the Forest

Hester Prynne was eager to tell Reverend Dimmesdale all about Chillingworth. But she did not want to go to his house. She knew that he often took long walks alone in the woods. So for several days she went out looking for him. But she had no success in finding him.

Then one morning Hester heard someone say that Dimmesdale had gone to spend the night at a nearby Indian village. So the next day, she set out to meet him on his return through the forest. When she heard him coming, she sent Pearl to play by the brook. Then she called out the minister's name, softly at first, then louder.

"Who is that?" said Dimmesdale. His face looked as if he had lost the desire to live. He looked worn out. He was holding his hand over his heart. As he came a few steps closer, he said, "Hester? Hester Prynne? Is it you?"

"Yes, Arthur," she said. "And you—have you found peace?"

Dimmesdale remained silent. He took Hester's hand in his own cold hand. He led her into the shadow of the woods. When they came to a bank of moss beside a brook, they sat down. Finally Dimmesdale answered Hester's question. "Not peace, no—nothing but pain and sadness. What else could I expect, being a man of God?"

"But all the people of Boston love and respect you," said Hester. "Doesn't this bring you any comfort?"

"Only greater misery," answered the minister with a bitter smile. "Every Sunday in church the people look up at me and listen to my words. It's as if they expect to see the light of heaven beaming from my face. Nobody knows about the evil in my heart. Hate is what I deserve! How can a ruined soul like mine hope to save other souls?"

"You judge yourself too harshly," said

Hester. "Your good works have long since made up for your sin."

"No, Hester, *no*!" replied the minister. "My work is cold and dead and can do nothing for me. Hester, you are lucky to be wearing the scarlet letter openly. Mine burns in secret. If only I had one friend—or even an enemy—to whom I could confess my sins every day. Even this much honesty and truth would save me."

Hester looked at the minister. She was almost afraid to tell Dimmesdale what she was about to say. But she had already made up her mind. "You have long had such an enemy," she said. "And you've lived with him under the same roof!"

The minister jumped to his feet, gasping for breath. He put his hand on his heart. "What are you saying?" he cried. "An *enemy*? And under my own roof! What do you mean?"

Hester stood up and faced him. "The doctor—Roger Chillingworth—he was my husband!" said Hester. Then she went on to tell Dimmesdale all about the doctor, and why she had been unable to speak before now.

For a moment the minister looked at her in surprise and anger. Then he sank down on the ground and buried his face in his hands. "I might have known it!" he said quietly. "I *did* know it! Wasn't my heart trying to tell me this from the first moment I met him? Why did I not understand? Hester, you have no idea of the horror of this thing! And the shame! *You* are to blame for this, Hester! I cannot forgive you!"

"You shall forgive me!" cried Hester. She threw herself down on the fallen leaves beside Dimmesdale. "Let God punish! You shall forgive!" she said. Then she threw her arms around him and pressed his head against her. She didn't mind that his cheek rested on the scarlet letter.

"Will you forgive me?" she softly whispered again and again.

Finally, Dimmesdale said, "I do forgive you, Hester. May God forgive us both. We are not the worst sinners in the world. There is one who is much worse."

For a long time, the two sat side by side,

holding hands. "Hester," said the minister, "do you think Roger Chillingworth will keep our secret? And how am I to live, breathing the same air as this deadly enemy?"

"You must not stay any longer with this evil man," said Hester. "Your heart must no longer be under his evil eye! You must go far away, across the sea. In Europe you would be beyond his power. You can begin again. The future can be full of happiness. Trade this false life of yours for a true one. Preach! Write! Act! Do anything except lie down and die! Change your name to one that you can use without fear or shame."

For a brief moment, a spark of life flashed in Dimmesdale's eyes. But it quickly died away. Sadly, he said, "Hester, I haven't enough strength or courage left to go into the world alone! I must die here."

"But you shall not go alone!" Hester whispered.

Now a look of hope and joy shone in Arthur Dimmesdale's face. "Is it really possible, Hester? Do I feel joy again?" he cried. "Why didn't we decide this sooner?"

"Let us not look back," answered Hester. "The past is gone. Why dwell on it now? Look—all I need do is remove this." As she spoke, she undid the pin that fastened the scarlet letter to her dress. Then she threw the letter into a pile of dry leaves.

Hester looked at Dimmesdale as another happy thought came to her. "You must get to know Pearl!" she said. "*Our* little Pearl! She is a strange child. But you will love her dearly, as I do."

"Do you think the child will be glad to know me?" he asked uncertainly.

"Yes, she will love you," said Hester with a smile. "She is not far off. I will call her. Pearl! Pearl!"

Pearl had been playing on the other side of the nearby brook. When she heard her mother calling her, she came running. But when she saw the minister, she slowed down. Then she stopped. Suddenly the silence of the forest was broken by Pearl's wild screams and shrieks. The little girl was stamping on the ground and pointing her finger at Hester.

"I know what troubles the child," said Hester. "Children do not like any change in the things they are used to. Pearl misses something that she has always seen me wear!" Sadly, Hester picked up the scarlet letter from the ground and fastened it to her dress. "Do you know your mother now, child?" she said.

Pearl grew quiet right away. She came running over to Hester and threw her arms around her. "Now you are my mother, and I am your little Pearl!" She kissed Hester on both cheeks, and then kissed the scarlet letter, too.

"That was not kind of you," said Hester. "You show me a little love, and then you make fun of me!"

"Why is the minister sitting here?" asked Pearl. "Tell me!"

"He is waiting to greet you," Hester said. "He loves you, my little Pearl. And he loves your mother, too. Will you love him?"

"Does he love us?" said Pearl. "Will he go back with us, hand in hand, we three together, into the town?"

"Not now, dear child," answered Hester. "But soon he will walk hand in hand with us. We will have a home of our own. And you shall sit upon his knee. He will teach you many things and love you dearly. You will love him, won't you?"

"And will he always keep his hand over his heart?" asked Pearl.

"Foolish child, what kind of question is that!" said Hester. "Come over to him!"

But Pearl would not come. Her mother had to pull her over to the minister. Dimmesdale bent down and gave the child a kiss. At that, Pearl broke away from her mother and ran back to the brook. She bent over and dipped her face in the water, as if to wash away the kiss.

Then she stood alone by the brook, watching her mother and the minister. They were busy talking, making their plans.

# The New England Holiday

10

Arthur Dimmesdale looked back as he left the forest. There they were, Hester and Pearl. In her gray robe, Hester was standing next to a tree. Near her, Pearl was dancing along the stream. So the minister had *not* fallen asleep and dreamed!

Quickly, Dimmesdale walked on. His meeting with Hester had given him new energy. He thought about the plans he and Hester had made. A ship had arrived in the harbor. In four days it was to sail for Bristol, England. Hester knew the captain of the ship. In secret she would book passage for herself, Pearl, and Dimmesdale. Soon, the day after Election Day, they would sail off to a new life—a fresh start across the sea!

Now Dimmesdale had work to do. He needed to finish writing the sermon he would give for the new governor on election day. This day was a great holiday in New England. It was an honor for Reverend Dimmesdale to give the sermon. He wanted to leave Boston knowing he had done his job to the best of his ability.

When Dimmesdale arrived home, the apartment and everything in it looked different. Then he realized that the change was within *him*, not the apartment. He was no longer the same person who had lived and suffered here for the past seven years. There on the table was the half-written sermon he had begun two days ago. The man he *used to be* had written it. Now that person was gone!

Just then there was a knock at the door. "Come in," said Dimmesdale. When the door opened, old Roger Chillingworth walked in. Dimmesdale immediately put his hand over his heart.

"And how was your visit at the Indian village?" asked the old doctor. "Sit down. You are looking pale. Surely you will need my help to make you strong enough to give the sermon on election day."

"No, I don't think so," said the minister. "My walk in the fresh air of the forest has done me good. I will not have need of your drugs, my friend."

Chillingworth gazed at Dimmesdale, studying him carefully. The young minister saw a strange smile on the doctor's face. He was afraid the old man knew that Hester had told him everything. If so, there was no telling what he might be planning now.

Soon the doctor left the minister's apartment. Dimmesdale picked up the pages of the sermon he had already written and threw them into the fire. Then he sat down to write a new sermon. Now he was bursting with happy ideas and feelings. The words flowed from his heart and onto the paper. He worked all night. When the golden rays of dawn came through the windows, the pen was still in his hand.

In the early morning hours of election day, a crowd was already gathering in the marketplace. Hester and Pearl walked through the crowd. Pearl was dressed in bright colors. Hester wore her usual gray dress and the scarlet letter. As usual, her outward look was calm and serious. But inside she was burning with excitement. Soon she would be far away from here.

Pearl noticed lots of strangers in the crowd—mostly Indians and sailors. With their colorful clothing and strange ways of speaking, they stood out in the Puritan crowd. Pearl was drawn to them. Dancing around the strangers like a butterfly, she asked her mother why they were all here.

"They've come to hear the music and watch the parade," said Hester.

"Will the minister be there?" asked Pearl. "Will he greet me, as he did by the brook in the forest?"

"Yes, he will be there, child," answered Hester. "But he will not greet you today— nor must you greet him."

"What a strange, sad man he is, with his hand always over his heart!" said Pearl.

"Be quiet, Pearl! You do not understand these things," said her mother. "Do not think about the minister now. Look around you at all these happy faces, my little Pearl."

At that moment, on the other side of the marketplace, Dr. Chillingworth was talking to the captain of the ship. Later, the ship's captain came up to Hester. "So, mistress," he said. "I must get ready one more cabin than we had agreed upon. We won't have to worry about scurvy or fever on this trip! Besides our own ship's doctor, we also have another doctor!"

"Why, what do you mean?" asked Hester, trying to hide her surprise. "Have you another passenger?"

"Do you not know that this doctor—Chillingworth, he calls himself—plans to sail with us?" said the captain. "He tells me he is one of your group. And he says he is a close friend of the gentleman you spoke of!"

Just then, Hester saw Chillingworth across the marketplace. He was smiling at her. She did not like the look of that evil smile. Before she could think of what to do, she heard the sound of music. The parade was about to begin.

Soon the marching band went by,

followed by straight columns of soldiers. Then came the judges, governors, and other officials. Last of all came Reverend Dimmesdale. Today he looked strong and tall. He walked with steady steps, and his hand was not over his heart.

Without even a glance in Hester's direction, Dimmesdale walked proudly by. Could this be the same man she had just felt so close to in the forest? She felt sad that he seemed so far away from her. Her spirits sank at the thought that she must have been fooling herself. How could there ever be a bond between her and the minister?

A voice next to Hester said, "Could you tell, Hester Prynne, that he is the same man you spoke with in the forest?" Hester quickly turned around. It was the old witch, Mistress Hibbins.

"I'm sure I don't know what you're talking about," said Hester.

"Hester!" said the old woman. "I've been to the forest so many times that I can always tell who has been there. What is it that the minister seeks to hide, with his hand always over his heart? Soon enough, the Devil will make his servant reveal his secret to the whole world!" The old woman gave a shrill laugh that sent chills down Hester's spine.

Before Hester could say another word, Mistress Hibbins had disappeared into the crowd. By now Reverend Dimmesdale had reached the church. The crowd of people followed him inside.

11 The Confession

Hester stood next to the scaffold as Reverend Dimmesdale began his sermon. She could hear his voice through the walls of the church. Although she couldn't make out his words, she could tell that his message was powerful and moving. His voice shook with strong feelings. At times he seemed to be crying out with guilt, begging for God's forgiveness!

As still as a statue, Hester listened to the whole sermon. The minister's voice drew her like a magnet. As she stood there, a group of people gathered around her, staring at the scarlet letter on her dress. Although these people were mostly strangers, they had all heard about her.

Once again, Hester was overcome with shame. She felt as if the scarlet letter was burning her skin. She thought about Dimmesdale. Inside the church, the people were all looking up to him with love and admiration. And here she was, the woman of the scarlet letter, standing in the market-place! No one could have imagined that the same sin was on both their souls.

The sermon finally ended. For a moment there was silence inside the church. People had been deeply moved by the minister's words. Heading back toward the town hall, people were talking about what Reverend Dimmesdale had said. Many of them said it was the greatest sermon they had ever heard. Never had any minister spoken in so wise and holy a spirit!

When the crowd saw Dimmesdale in their midst, their shouts died down to a whisper. Their dear minister did not look at all well. He was very pale, and he seemed to be having trouble walking. The Reverend Wilson offered his arm, and Governor Bellingham rushed up to help him. But Dimmesdale waved them aside. He turned toward the scaffold and stopped beside Hester and little Pearl.

Stretching out his arms, Dimmesdale cried out, "Hester Prynne, come here! Come, my little Pearl!"

The child flew to him, throwing her arms about his knees. Hester slowly drew near. Then suddenly, old Roger Chillingworth pushed through the crowd. He caught Dimmesdale by the arm.

"*Madman!*" the old doctor whispered. "What are you trying to do? Keep that woman and child away. Do not ruin your good name! I can yet save you!"

"Devil!" cried Dimmesdale. "I think you are too late! Your power is not what it was! With God's help, I will escape you now!"

Again he held out his hand to the woman of the scarlet letter. "Hester Prynne, come help me reach the scaffold!"

The crowd was so taken by surprise that they stood staring. Silent, they saw their minister climb the steps of the scaffold. Leaning on Hester's shoulder, he held Pearl's little hand in his own. Following just behind them was Roger Chillingworth.

Chillingworth said to Dimmesdale,

"There is no place in the world that you could have escaped me, Dimmesdale! Except on this very scaffold!"

"Thank God who has led me here!" said the minister. Turning to Hester with a weak smile, he said, "Isn't this better than what we had planned in the forest? God is merciful. Hester, I am a dying man. Let me hurry to take my shame upon me!"

Dimmesdale, still leaning on Hester and holding Pearl's hand, turned to the crowd. "People of New England," he cried in a loud voice. "You who have loved me and thought me holy—look at me, a sinner. At last I stand on the spot where I should have stood seven years ago. Look at the scarlet letter which Hester wears. You have turned away from her. But there was someone else here that you should have turned away from!"

Dimmesdale was growing weaker, but he forced himself to go on. "One who lived among you kept his own scarlet letter hidden. Hester's scarlet letter is just a shadow of the mark he wears on his own chest! God's eye saw it. The angels pointed at it. The Devil knew it well. But this man kept it hidden from people. Now look at how God judges a sinner!"

With a quick motion, Dimmesdale opened his shirt. There were gasps of horror in the crowd. Then the minister fell down on the scaffold. Hester cradled his head in her arms. Chillingworth bent down beside him. "You have escaped me!" he kept repeating. "You have *escaped* me!"

"May God forgive you, Chillingworth," said the minister. "You, too, have sinned."

Then he turned to the woman and child. "My little Pearl," he said weakly. There was a sweet and gentle smile on his face. "Will you kiss me now? You wouldn't kiss me in the forest, but will you now?"

Pearl kissed his lips. A spell was broken as her tears fell upon her father's cheek. Because her father had been named, Pearl would not grow up wild. She would not have to fight the world. She would be able to feel human joy and sorrow. She would be a woman in the world.

"Hester," said the minister, "farewell!"

"Shall we not meet again? Will we not be together in heaven?" asked Hester. "What do you see for us?"

"God alone knows, Hester—but we know He is merciful! His will be done! Farewell!" The final word came with the minister's dying breath. The crowd, silent until then, broke out in a strange, deep voice of wonderment.

After many days had passed, people had thought about and talked over what they had seen. They wanted to understand what had happened. But there were several different ideas about what had actually been seen on the scaffold that day.

Most of the people believed they had seen a scarlet letter on the minister's chest. Some thought he had tortured himself to make the letter. Some thought that old Roger Chillingworth had caused it to appear by the use of magic or drugs. Others said the letter had been made by the minister's guilt. And then there were some people who had seen no letter. There were even some who felt that Dimmesdale had not confessed to being guilty of any sin.

Nothing was stranger than the change that took place in Roger Chillingworth. Soon after Reverend Dimmesdale's death, the old doctor seemed to dry up. He was like an uprooted weed that lies wilting in the sun. For too long his life had been driven by his need for revenge. Once Dimmesdale was gone, the doctor's life was empty. He had nothing to live for. He died within a year.

When he died, Chillingworth left a great deal of property to Pearl. She became rich. Shortly thereafter, Hester and Pearl left Boston. Then, many years later, Hester returned to Boston to live in her old cottage. She still wore the scarlet letter!

Now and again Hester would receive letters from another country. These were believed to be letters from Pearl, who was said to be married and happy.

Hester had her reasons for returning to Boston. Life had more meaning here than in the strange country where Pearl had found a home. Here in Boston had been Hester's sin, and here her sorrow.

Over the remaining years of her life Hester helped many young women. When they had problems, they came to Hester's cottage, and she would always give comfort and advice. As for Hester, she wore the scarlet letter for the rest of her life!

After many, many years, a new grave was dug, near an old and sunken one in the cemetery near King's Chapel. Hester Prynne was to be buried beside Arthur Dimmesdale. One stone was used for both graves. On the stone was a scarlet letter A.